T0328519

A PILE OF MIXED EMOTIONS

by

THABANG MPELE

Bhiyoza Publishers (Pty) Ltd

A Pile of Mixed Emotions

Bhiyoza Publishers (Pty) Ltd

Johannesburg, South Africa

Bhiyoza Publishers (Pty) Ltd
PO Box 1139
Ridgeway
2099

Email: info@bhiyozapublishers.co.za
www.bhiyozapublishers.co.za

First edition, first impression 2020
ISBN: 978-1-990940-02-6 – A pile of mixed emotions

Cover design: Suide-Wolde Digital (Pty) Ltd
Layout and typeset: Suide-Worlde Digital (Pty) Ltd

ACKNOWLEDGEMENT

My special thanks to Dr Mothofela Msimanga, for giving me the platform to present everything and shine, for his patience, his contribution and dedication to make this book a success.

Thabang Mpele
2019

TABLE OF CONTENTS

No.	Contents	Page No.

1   With you

I conquered my fears.
As you drop down tears
You taught me how to fight
Without using sharpened spears.
With you,
I learnt how to be patient
I swear it was like I was pregnant
Months went by with you kickin'
Inside my heart as I
Travelled all the doctors
Asking why you're kickin' this hard
Ass ripped, couldn't ever fart.
As you turned inside my heart
My chest stumbled
Only nipples remained constant.
With you
I felt like a participant
In all sports scenes
Played in soft grounds green.
Wondering now, where you've been.
With you,
I used to laugh
And also be happy as
I tell you what, you were…
You were my light.
But now with you again
We've aborted an innocent soul
Left in a tiny bottle of foul

Pretence has become our vow
Your heart that kicked with mine
Has now suddenly stopped beating
Not even my month can pour out
Our running words of sorrow,
Only the bullets you threw
Went straight to my eyes.
With you,
I felt not comforted
Even though we stood there
Alone at the Airport,
To say our last parting words,
Our last goodbyes, love
Tears ran out in my eyes
Words cracked in my ears
I retrieved my fears
That when I am with you I conquer.
With you,
Life was better then
But now I taste only bitterness
Yet I wish you great joy, love
And swear never to be treated like toys
And I hope you sit and knob a tie.
And welcome kissing strangers
Coz you no longer exist.
Dead!
Extinct!

^2 Alone

Left people and chose to be with you
Left home to be near you
Travelled a rough road with you,
Led by fake characters
I burnt bridges
Only to find no seas,
Stood by you, strike my fears
Our love was behind the scenes
Only to find out it was a long film
Played behind higher mountains
Stood with you in rains
Left my heart unattended,
Let the feeling of allurement
Take-over,
Now it's over.
Am left alone
Holding on to the crippled mountains,
Crushed by the rains.
Am slowly tumbling down,
I thought I had found my own,
But no, it was a temporary crown,
Tried catering it as unfriendly
Weathers blew it,
But I remained alone.
A soul tormented
A heart foul cremated
Tears left the face cemented

Left a hanging body
With ripped clothes
Showing white bones
With skin tried cloning
You store my heart, conning.
Alone in the area
Where there's no place of earing
Could hear my phone ringing.
Spent nights slowly
Tumbling down,
Cried myself to see sleep,
With pillows as my sweep.
I loved you, only you,
Faithful I remained, but in
The end I stood
Alone. Alone. Alone.

3   Secretively

Faked your smiles
As I meant miles
Travelled with you a distance
But came with disturbance
My heart freed-up and beat-up for you
By you, I stood firm
Secretively we dated
Publicly we were rated
Publicity led by fake characters
None could be faithful actresses,
Can't believe I jumped puddles
To be with you in the rattles
I tried holding to opinions
But my feelings remained intact,
I gave you my all never as an act.
Secretively you loved me
But publicly you denied me
Secretively you're my muse
My worst destruction
And if that's what you want
Secrete love
Am ready to give you all
Secretly
Secretively.

4 Answers

Answers reminiscing in my mind
Answers circulating over my thoughts:
Should I agree to this situation?
Should I take myself out of this misery?
Should I be patient?
But for how long can I do that?
Questions popped as pop-corns being fried.
I resent the fact that he lied
And there I was as I foolishly I cried
All he maybe saw a friend
But he could've been specific
Yes I am scientific
Born to rock the mountains
And survive through rains
Neither without you or with you
See all you have is your pride
And you want me to be your bride
But see the plane that we'll ride
May take away your life
And you'll die alive.
Answers are with me
I'll stay for I desire to
But your theories
Are untold stories
You're a perfect liar
But answers lie behind your heart
The red key resists, the heart!

5   How am I?

As mind fickle with rumbling
Shaming answers,
Afraid of denial
Afraid of loneliness
Comforted by lies
It's been my life
And it's never been live
Not even on our televisions
My life can be only visions
Nothing like beauty pageants
Nobody can make agreements
And I only can make amendments
Who am I?
They've played me
And I know how being
Hurt feels like
It's rare for people to
Envy for it
I have made
Choices that nobody
Would've chosen
For they are like ghost chase
My life played like a story
And this time what amazes
Me is that the characters
Were the trees
Audience were the natural features,
I'm simply invisible
Story, drama, this is who I am.
Half of me.

6   Caught up

I'm caught up
In a rocky situation
And I can find no solution
Laying on the rugged ground
Hoping that maybe you'll come around
As many thoughts circulated
And I kept on counted
Time went by
Since it waits for no body
Two options were there
And I accounted you to be here
But nothing like you
Ever showed up,
Stood up as I heard
Crawls of screams
Only to find a crown of virtuous lion,
Showed up your face.
Is it too late or should I run,
But where to?
Caught up
Between a crown of vultures,
Or a river to wipe away my fears,
As they shifted proudly
Made their way towards me,
My body shook,
One option caught up
Should I throw myself in?
Or should I drown myself?
Caught up in your love,
I resist to drown......

7 Fallen apple

Beauty was what you were
He exchanged his glistering eyes
To you
As your mind got confused
He stretched his gold arm
Towards you,
As you lowered yourself
To reach to him,
You gave him up your life
He took you with care
Of which in your life was rare
He spoke the honey words you wanted to hear,
As you froze into his coldness
But you showed him kindness
Fallen apple
You were everyone's envy
You fell in the hands of a selfish man
He cut you, sliced you
A bit by bit poor soul
The pain you felt as he took
Away your beauty
And you wished to go back
But all of that was impossible
You thought he'll treat you well
But he never even knew that word,
Fallen apple fell on the wrong selfish-hands
Of a man who was cruel

Fallen apple
Fallen apple
Grew to become beautiful
But never thought you'd be a fool
Nothing to you was ever a foul
Proof you never stopped
Glowing even in darkest nights
Your greenest soul kept
Growing and growing
You were far at the
Highest part of the tree
Farmers came and took
The others left at you
Since none of them could
Reach up to you
Not even their tools
You were just one juicy thing
Your freshness glowed in
Their eyes, nobody has
Tried to catch.
You fallen apple
Were able to survive
All the stones thrown at you
Even when the tree had become wounded
But you were resilient,
You remained at your highest
Until one man charmed you
Spoke all the juicy words
You've always wished to hear,
Since all they ever did

Was to swear at you
And that's all you wore
Their swearing's, poor fallen apple.

8   Your voice

As he greets me
My cheeks couldn't hold
Themselves anymore
As I mumbled
Hands came to my rescue,
Waves passed near him,
As he shook with fear
And you've putted your gear
Uttered sweet words,
As you froze on his world,
He came nearer
As I hesitated to leave
"But a few minutes wouldn't hurt",
Said the mind as ears heard,
"Can I give you my number?"
That's all he said, to my slumber
As my hands uncontrollably
Passed him my Nokia Asha,
His voice kept playing on my ears,
As he transferred to me his fears.
We departed there
As my face glistered,
Day went by and only
Your face was playing in my thoughts
I tried to resist them, by force
But your voice played a song
My ears persisted to listen

Your voice so sweet
Took away my feelings
To my you were eyes appealing
Your charming voice
Gave me no choice but to text you immediately,
Your voice so sweet.

9   Being in love with you

Being with you
It's supposed to be a thrill
But it all recuperate to be a kill
Nobody has it than you, as your skill
It's supposed to be a sweet dream
Said Beyoncé as she indulged
With saying beautiful nightmares
It started all good
And it is what people admire,
And that wasn't one of our desires,
Being in love with you
Feels like being lost
On a veld that has no way-out
And again it's never easy
For you to leave,
Since it's admirable and comfortable
I could have left if I were able to,
But being in love with you
Tires my knees constantly
And I pay no attention to fools,
My love for you runs like water
In the pools of abundance,
Flooded with nails and spikes
And covered in pains
Is being in love with you.
Is not an easy task
But I can't quit no more,
Being in love with you.
Because I am in love with you.

The heart wants what it wants

The heart wants what it wants.
Said a man who misused the words
With a purpose to justify his phase,
For he knew no grace at all
Nor did he understand mercy
For all he was, was a mess.
Melting around human shaped finders
Nothing like the keepers.
Balls rolled to friendly grass
But it would never last
The man grabbed apples
On a blooming tree,
But again his spirit gasps
For oranges on yellow dreams
His handsomeness made lemons
As his personality was full of demons
Bees surrounded his skinny body
As he ate his honey
Hi! I am lonely love
My eyes said to him,
As his body shook with lust
Beauty was all he saw
The heart pounded and said to him
"I want what I want now"
I wonder why it didn't say:
"Leave that, for it's not yours"
Coz all the man did

Ended like mist
He misused the phrase
For he was weak to face his phase
He said, "The heart wants what it wants"
Yes, he misused the phrase for lust.

11 Sour

The taste of your personality
Was full of fantasy of reality.
Red velvet now our sour porridges
Red devil there to polish our ridges
Your body bought sexual appellate
My body glanced at your super ability
And it was with that probability
You were strong and knew your plan
I was weak and got to be your fan
You gave me your taste
I gave you my waste
You sucked all the taste out of me
Real devil you walked with your spade
It got too late for me to fade
You had me eternally shamed
Vulnerability got the best of me
And it was never too late
For me to go back to your crawl
I had turned to be your owl
Held to you hoped to be your all
But things changed
And all I could taste
Was your bitterness
Your bitter dirtiness
Your salty sweat and sadness
Sourness was all over the places I licked
Now I don't like them no more.
Sour taste is what you've became.
Bad taste! Frustration.

12   What you said

What you said left me vast
I never thought my breath will last
As you found your way fast
I'm trying to let go of the past
I wait no more my love
For what you said was too raw, crude
Never mind that it's still in the law
Stupidity then ruled me
You've deceived me
You played me like a piano
You said you'll wait for me
But no, that was a lie
Contemplated in a shoebox
That had your scent
Which drove me insane
I kept inhaling it once
My jacket held your scent
Missing you was a waste
Of feelings lost and wasted
Crying for you was a waste
Of my tears and lost hope
Fighting for you was like
Fighting a losing battle
Loving you was only a key to pain
What you said left me ashamed
I felt dead, I felt stupid
But I waited no more
For I'm done being your fool.
What you said is forgiven now
Hope you live a good life, lover.

13   Alone in the place of darkness

Alone in darkness where light shine no more,
A journey leads me to this secrete dark place
Where no human can enter this darkness,
Where animals go missing in this darkness,
Where plants get greener day by day
Cold as a deep-freezers in this darkness.
Mist is the only air occupying the field
Stones covered with grass in darkness
Water freezes seemly as a glass in darkness
Only footsteps were the sound
Trees sang melodies in darkness
As droplets of water formed a beat
Lyrics were formed out of breath
As I breathe in and out heavily
Cheeks frozen till turned red in darkness
Shoe covered with mud, turned brown
Pants wet from the grasses waters
The night was only what I saw
For I knew no day in this darkness
As I continued with my journey
Sleep on unfriendly grass
But I hope to last in this darkness
Days went by as my stomach filled only
With river water in the dark
Alone in the darkness I grope
Only your picture was visible
Played on my mind in the dark

As my favourite song bleated in the dark
Alone is what I want to be in darkness
I'd appreciate if you'd disappear in the dark
Form my eyes, for you're the light and shines
And I shall adapt to the situation that shines…
I am alone in the darkness where never shine

14   Gates

As wind blew stronger
My eyes couldn't see no more
As I ran to the nearest place
Only your home was the one I could reach
But I never wanted to enter there
Winds blew faster and stronger
Roof tops flew like birds in the sky
Cars moved carefully, slowly as cats to eat rats
My heart sank in the muddy place
That I was standing at the gate
It wasn't even a metre away from your gate
As the car spun uncontrollably
My mind snapped out of the dream
Hands shook as they held your gate
But it was locked and hard to unlock
It came directly with its ugly face
And threw me inside your yards
Loud noise, is what I could remember
Gate was the only picture I could retrieve
Gate had my life, but it decided to give life away
Only life knew why.
Gate.

15   Rain swept my tears

Rain washed away my sorrow
Rain covered my wet face
As my clothes became heavy
My mind delivered unsettling thoughts
As my knees shook faster because of coldness
My eyes turned sour, and sure they were red.
My hands holding down on sharp stones
I lift them up to wipe me face
But it became bloody and tired
Rain washed my blood away
My heart sank as floods pushed my helpless body
Into a veld of desolate and frustration.
All I could remember, were my hopeless screams
"Help! Help!" were the only words uttered
I saw you, you let the rain pushed me
You stood there and did nothing to help
The rain washed my dirt away
But left me hurt and frustrated.
Were you standing because you had no choice?
Or you just enjoyed all that scene?
The rain carried all the wrong thoughts to my heart.
Sinking sheep, is what I was love.
I floated like a helpless dead body
"You never cared", I assumed.
But still my brain is corrupted by your love
The rain sifted my love for you
And it all makes sense now
That it is love on the brain.
Rain!

16   Enough

It's enough
Your heart has unrepairable holes
It has bled and been hurt enough already!
Enough!
Listen to the inner you
Don't let the emotions take over
It's enough!
Your face is pale because of the floods
That you've been excreting out of your eyes!
Enough!
Listen to the inner you.
Wipe away all that rain on your face
It's enough!
Enough is enough!
Take a stand! Be bold!
Stand tall; shake all the dust off.
Enough is enough!
You can't be holding onto hopeless people
Yet there's a shiny future above you
It may be all sort of emotional
But don't let that take over
Claim your worth
Enough is enough!
I've heard it all
Seen it all, I am done!
I'm claiming my throne!
Enough is enough!
Enough.

17   The day that went by

My eyes set straight
Straight into the street
As my feet refuse to walk
Hands can't stop holding my phone
As I hoped your name will appear
On my screen and rejoice.
But you're nowhere to be seen
As I sat an my bed with wet eyes
Hanged with sadness at the window
Hoping to see your shadow
Ears sharpened to hear your knock
Hands clutching the cellphone
Feet carried me outside now and then
Cos you're driving my mind insane
Let alone as my body becomes heavy
The day went by with longing
Sun-flared and unrevealed,
Everything within me ached
And the day consistently went by.

18   Who are you?

As beautiful morning
Streets shining and glowing
Filled with cars and people swinging
My feet carrying me with boldness
As I walk faster with boldness
And my eyes became brighter
Yet my soul remained darker
As your voice uttered my name
My heart was excited
When my mouth was kissed
My eyes lit because of pleasure
Yet my feet longed to leave
But my mind and curiosity ruled
And so my body without patience remained
Who are you?
Asked my doubting heart
As it vowed and concluded
That you're to be somebody I know not
Your shivering made me wonder
The day went by as the question
Remained, who are you?

I'm so sorry

I'm so sorry again
I got all worked up
Maybe I was just made up
I pushed you away
And see I did that without acknowledging
All I wished was for you
To see my value and love
But instead I shove you away
I shove you like dirt
A lot of grammatical errors done
I'm so sorry love, I am sorry
All I ask from you is forgiveness
I still do care a lot and not less
I still love you much and care
I still want you next to my face
I still want to know you better
I'm sorry love, I am sorry
I was driven by vile thoughts
And now my heart bleeds regret
Although I had every right to be mad
But I can't get over you.
I'm so sorry love, I am sorry
Please come back to me now
This time I promise to love you internally
I promise to love you unconditionally
I'm so sorry love, I am sorry
I never meant to break your heart

I just wished for one thing
But I ruined the great love we had.
Please come back to me now
I'm sorry love, I am sorry
You're my energy and source of inspiration

20 Sometimes

You may not matter to a person
You thought you mean the world,
Where is he at you lowest?
When I always assumed he's the best.
And at that time he was all I saw, delusion
My mind too stagnant to remove his image.
Never mind his age, the mirage.
He was and still in my heart.
He's is one drug that I'm addicted to,
My mind and heart are in a battle,
One claims I'm done with him,
The other has the virtuous power to say
"I'm not over him yet"
Maybe as time goes by
He'll realise that I only wanted the best
Out of what we had.
Love-sick idiots and are persistent
About "love conquers all"
But forgetting that "love has demands and
scarifies"
Who knew that I can make you lose your
mind?
Who knew I'll be crazy about you?
The he that I thought will always be by me.
He's now gone, without a fight
The he that I love

Am I alive or dead?

As I said you brought back my passion
But you're taking me to prison
Our love, lit
As my eyes became blurred
Mind and body where are you?
My clothes hanging over the roof
Am I alive or dead?
I need proof of life
You claimed to love me
And yet I think you're using me
Am I alive or dead?
My lips carried by a wheelbarrow
Are they that heavy?
What's the hurry?
As my body followed in a catch
I ask: Am I alive or dead?
I'm always in pains
Pains that have became
My daily bread
Sad love and stressful sex are now us.
Yet love has become bitter.
Your body burns fire
And now I am burning
Watch me burn to death
Watch me break into bones
Watch my meat turn into dry animal skin
Watch my bones turn into ashes
Am I alive dead?
Coz I don't feel my worth anymore
I might as well be no more

²² You'll miss up

I'll be nowhere
To be found,
Your world may go
Round.
Yet I'll not be proud
As you'll walk with shame
Where will be your fame?
Keep on playing with me
Somebody will pick me
And see my worth
Maybe I'm wrong nor right
But my light shall shine bright
And yours will dim
As we will dine.
Mountains will move
As lightning and thunderstorms groove.
You'll miss me
And I'll be nowhere to be spotted
I give you my support, you're supported
I give you my all
But it seem as you're giving me your peace.
Thou we're moving in a fast pace.
And FYI I don't want your pieces.
If you can't give me your all
I don't want your parts.
You'll miss me
As we play hide and seek

Who are you hiding from?
Or am I shaming you?
"Welcome" will no longer exits
You'll miss me.

23   It's more like, who are you?

Friday swifts rapidly to Sunday
It is was like who are you
And it's like who are you
My heart never stops beating
And smiling upon the doors of heavens
Like who are you?
I had a slight better chance,
To know you well.
But am still wondering
Who are you?
People talk and judge,
They try to oblige
By asking unfriendly questions.
But all of this draws me passion
To love you stronger
And question myself repeatedly
Will I ever get to understand or
Be answered on this question?
Who are you?
You broke my heart to pieces
But you again mended it
I watched as you sew it
In your type of cotton
Warm and inviting
With a topping of comfort and caring
Like who are you?
Let you under my skin to suck my lipids

Passionate kisses on my poor lips
Never mind the question,
There's still time I'll figure
Orange juice within me rinse the cups.
The cups of my question-carriers.
Leaving taste to bubble up, the question,
That's more like who are you?
You fried my cardiac like chips.
Like person who are you?
Am puzzled like a piece of land.
Travelled the city you're my Rand.
Like who are you?
I opened this tool of love
Chapter four verse nine
Wish to see you now
And let you know how much I adore you
And assure you with my sweet words
That I'll never leave you
I rejuvenated everything I think of,
What you pulled to get through me
Who are you?
To take courage on
Chapter 2016 verse ten
To pull up your guts
And put up your fights
To dark streets,
You turned lights
And reminded me of my rights
Who are you?
Is it my mind that's crippled?

Or the question should remain
To be, "who are you?"
And now it's more like
Who are you?

24   Did I rush?

Did I rush to tell you that I love you?
Was I supposed to slow down and
Try to understand,
What love is?
Did I rush to grow up?
Or is it that I felt lonely?
Not that I blame situations
But I had my mother only
The void in my heart was great
Of having a father figure in my life
I couldn't ignore growing up
Did I rush or was it the time?
The time for me to experience
All that I ever wanted
Was to have a loving partner
And now all that is my anguish
Unfortunately we never get to choose
Who we fall in love with
Did I rush or the regret is taking its place?
Did I rush to be a rebellious young soul?
Who never took good advices of the adults?
Who never ever considered those?
For they lived their own young hood life?
And times have changed now
But one thing that never changes
This is what they reprimand us of
"Don't rush to date that will disturb your
education"
But all of this goes to waste

I mean who are they tell us about
reproduction
Where else we've our own ways
To get drugs to drown our soul
And move warm with our rags
Did I rush to love you?
To take in that smoke
And puff it to dirty the atmosphere?
Is it only fair now?
Since our fathers and mothers did it?
Why not we do it also?
Remember the reprimands from our parents
Who told us to stay away from love and
From our beloved friends?
Well they knew they could lead us astray
Did I rush to enjoy life?
But it's a "YOLO"
Why not get wasted
And never look for all the time gone?
And hang my hands on the phone.
Did I rush?
Or is it what we can do
Just what everyone does
Sitting, eating, chatting
Let me put it back
Is it rush of teens?
Why not crave for education?
Did I rush to get tired of books?
Did I rush to love you?
Did we rush?
Or did I rush?

25 It is me

It is still me
Who wore a Zulu attire?
And gave a speech to inspire
This is what I aspired to
To build a foundation
Of a steep poetry
More to overlap and be
A fountain bubbling
It is me who stood
In font of crowds
To cheer and own the crown
To move the sicknesses
And leave a new leaf
Of life
It is me
Who walked passed
The mob
Laughing at my walk
But I still; walked tall
Remained as high as I could
Never bowed for any human
This is how it should remain
Till to face my fate
And let it dance to my tune
This is my boldness
I'm the king of my own
My tears better renew

For I'm coming to destruct
It is me, who passed males
To mock at me
And call me a "faggot"
Now we love
At the corners
Secretly in the dark
Only rumours are true
And no action prevailed
For we are concurred
By the homophobes
Of this Earth
That feeds us only Self-doubt
And leave us
Self-less worth
I refuse to live a
Dictated life by
The people who hardly
Know how they feel
Nor one feels.
It is
It is the world
Of vultures
Full of many who are Vulnerable
It is
It is what I want
To be free
And live my own life
Without being judged and yes I will

The time has came

I never thought I'll weep
And wet my pillow
Feel this hopeless
Anything I touch turns to be
An object
For me to hold on to
And be reminded of you.
My green blanket
To rejuvenate my soul
And be reminded of our great times
My blue pillow
To open my sky
As I watch it play a scene
A pillow fight
With my body on my trap –bed
Rolling myself like a worm
Hoping my heart has won
A keeper to guard me
A lover to guide me
But now I have to accept
That the time has came
For us to say our goodbyes
I'll forever always love you
Distance won't mean a thing
But love shall keep our souls
Intertwined
Go well my sweetheart

I will always care
And I love you
The time for you to leave me has came
Go out there and shine
Go make me proud
And always be reminded
Welcome loves you

27   You and Me

You existed in my dream,
That I hoped won't come to an End
But as they say
"It all comes to an End"
Even the world on its own Shall End
You lived in my head
And in my mind and soul
Couldn't get more of you
Love, you gave me fantasy
Although sometimes it wasn't easy
We existed
You and me
We lived in our own cupped,
Small shining world
Facing the sky together
Swore to never departure
And now it's a torture
Imagining life with no you
That is like a death sentence
It becomes an essay
Will no full-meaning
You completed my life
There were no other
Other people in our eyes
It was you and me
Like birds on the wind
We flew with no worries

And like little kids,
Playing hide and seek,
We, shared all
Let's just say
It was a dream for you and me.

²⁸ I cry

As I fake a smile
Just to keep you a mile
Away so you won't notice
I'm just trying to give you my piece
About this journey
It is a journey of love
A small package
That consists of a baggage
It is not for weak hearts
Listen it's for real-hard-cores
As I sing this chorus
I cry my darling
Words describing my currency
I'm a wounded heart
I live by my scars
Watch as I escalate my fears
Losing you is my worst enemy
But in this game of love,
You'll need more than just energy,
You'll seek for your own remedy
I cry my darling
For I knew less
Thought it all goes sweet
Smoother and slippery like a jelly fish
But be aware those legs of it
Are a sword
To cut heart to small pieces

I cry my darling
For nobody warned me
Even if they did
I chose to be blind
And so I cry my darling

I cannot

Is see your face
Every time I fade ...
To sleep eternally
I see your glowing smile
That shines my mood
And kills all planted weed,
As that smoke...
Travels through pipeline,
Of my nostrils
And makes me dizzy
Feel your presence in my loneliness
You're that fizzy lollipop
That I cannot get enough of
I cannot get angry
Nor mad at you for a decade of time
It is said
"Like the sand through the hour glass, so are
the days of our lives"
See you're the glass
That allows me to see the sand
As it dries to be soul
And turns to dust that,
When it cools I see my future flows
And so is my life
And its days on Earth to glister
I cannot get enough
Of your voice

I swear I'll always rejoice
Whenever it escalates my ears
My darling
I cannot see a future without you
Or say it is dull without you in the picture
For now let's play this movie and not feature
Coz I cannot share you
I cannot sleep, once we fight
You're my sword
To all my wars
So let's pour this love
To each other and never stop
Till the end of time.

30   **Blind**

My eyes full of mist
And you're on top of my call list
Trying to make a conversation
But this is a game to our generation
This and more penetrating
Blessers deal with trading
But in this case of love
Or said to be perpetuating
Full of blast lies
That turns a grey eye
My life taken for a gamble
As one picks it up for ruffle
Tried to keep quite
But this has to be heard
It is all over my head
A daily phrase: "love is blind"
Only those with great experience
Give out this for a raise
Opinionated some say
"It blinds everyone"
But I never thought that ...
That I'm also one of them
Grey mist
Grey decisions, blurry visions,
Empty future,
"Without him I'm nothing"
Words of those blinded by love

I refuse to be blind anymore
Maybe in another planet I'll be,
But for now
I'm refusing to be blind

A trembling heart

The sun gave off its heat
The raindrops created a beat
As my soul dances to the rhythm
This is my home of pain
The crib of sadness
Only known of greatness
Waves of air
Created a sweet sound
A sound of peace
That only my heart
Longs for
Food of soul
A rifting heart
That knows no happiness
That carriers burdens
All cupped with broken pieces
A dark pit
To throw off my imaginations
A cloud of light
That only gives grey storms
I'm crying out
For my heart
It knows no peace
It trembles when everyone's at peace
It only sleeps when it rains
For the sound creates a beat
It's not its favourite but it gives it peace
It is a trembling heart
That only envies peace

32   Set free

These chains are painful
These chains hold my heart
Cuffed like chicken feet
Set free
Hoping somebody would rescue it
Hoping one day it may be restored
It is my dream
To see it dance with pleasure
To beat and race in rain
It drowns in this pit pain
Set free
A crackly voice said,
Like a melody
To my ears
Trying to keep me out of my fears
Set me free yes,
It's been years
With this lump of chains
Bound to make grains
Out of my heart,
Panics my chest
For they're about to receive,
Sad news
This is only for a few
To grow and be bold
To face the fate
And watch as smoke fade
That would be when I'll say "it is set free"
For now set free

33   Secretly

Am in love with your smile
It glances from a mile
It shakes my mouth,
Words stumble to the floor
As my lips vibrate
For those words are powerful
My eyes blink
Due to not handling the glint
Tried showing my affection
As I pass your reflection
Wished for the same attraction
Let me clarify this,
My heart – beats for you
Changing directions
I hope to see this,
Our path destination
My road ends
At the corner of your house
As I move like a mouse
Help! My legs shook
As my eyes long to look,
At your image
My ears longing for your voice
My blood freezes like an ice
My heart jams,
In hope to stand time
Only a line...
In my head that I am ...
I am secretly in love with you

I am shaped for your heart

To throw in stones
At people's homes
Trying to manage the pain
Spinning in the rain
Hoping my love for you
Will drain
As I sweep water
With my shoes
And break the mother's rule
Looking around the universe
In hope to forget and reverse
Looking deeper in my life.
It's hard to admit that …
I am composed for your heart
Sipped cocktail and whiskey
Removing you from my mind
But in truth you're the key
To my heart, hard to find
Committed suicide a thousand times
But your love showers life in me
As I rise and make sound
Rejoicing for having you around
You're the chains
That I cannot escape
Played our dreamland tape
And remained not fake
You're my favourite subject

And I always object,
To make all rules you make
Well that's because
I am composed for your heart

Stuck

Suck up to my feelings
Stuck onto my dreams
Sick drowning in my fears
Sound so loud to my ears
Eat all up in my plate peas
Wandering 'round the garden peace
Left with only my soul
Tired of all the foul
Loved and denied
Swear my heart died
Stuck in frustration
Like sperm in a condom
To leave no condone
No child, no STI's
Rollin' in GTI's
Blessers
These harmful abusers
To bury their flaws
Buy them plenty of flowers
Gifts
Their coffins to be the last breath
HIV and AIDS
Life sentence jail
Pregnancy
Love to be a game
Lies
Killing of harmless

Abortion
This is all stuck
To the generation from
Penetration
This is all the crap
To our mothers wombs cramps

36   I'll hold on

As mountainous
And high as it may seem
I'll hold on
To reach my destination
This road is tough
And it's rough
As my feet are lazy to walk
And my mouth lazy to talk …
Words of wisdom
Only my ears
Hears the sound of birds
My body longing for my bed
My crackly lips craving for water
It's only beginning
It's about to be harder
Convinced my mind that …
It's only for a few days
But in reality it's of life time
My hands wounded,
From the stinging trees
I'll hold on
My road doesn't end here
That is what I need to hear
And comprehend
This is the time where I cry,
And be in need of a friend
Although it may seem hard

To accomplish my mission
I'll finish it for I have
A vision
And for that I'll hold on

37 Conquer

Wide opened the heavens doors
Ran upside down the doctors
An angel rose
Like a little fat flower
With its thick fleshy smile
Lightening up the atmosphere
We are really lucky to have you here
If it's meant to be it will be
See you're meant to conquer,
Every bitter situations
It's even in our eyes for recognition
You will ignite the spark
Of our souls
This bubbly personality
To receive our originality
You bring joy
To all the sour hearts
Your happiness
Burrows our wounds and heals 'em
You are really a conqueror
Your spirit and power of fighting things
Is really what some of us aspire
You're the light to the darkness
A bright shining little bulb
To a room of the poor
Let's just sum it all up
We're lucky to have,
Such a beautiful soul like you
Keep up the fighting spirit
Conqueror

Temptations

I've worn out my skin
To cover myself with your sins
Please forgive me for saying this
You're a temptation to my life
I was forced by your demons
To fulfil all your demands
"Resist! Resist! Resist!"
Said a tiny voice
That came deep in my soul
Pray! Pray! Pray!
The little girl in me said
But my lust took over,
 I craved for experiments
That came with all predicaments
This boy in me persisted
Our father who art in heaven …
But the grown man in me
Reminded me that it is him I love
Now that all that is gone
All the fantasy has faded away
And now I'm left with
Forgive us for our sins
And lead us not into temptations
I guess the devil
Used me a lot
Your demons devoured my soul
I'd swear you were heaven sent

You pushed all the right buttons
My friends were there to alert me
But I was blinded by your super-powers
But like I said
You were a temptation

39   This I know

I'm a coward
I don't want to come forward
To face my real demons
I'm a loner
Trying to engage in friendships
But my soul doesn't find peace
Trying to engage in relationships
I fail to keep up
For this I know
I demand attention
I want to feel appreciated
Fail to get enough of you
I try to make,
Every minute of life I spend
With you, a remarkable one
But I lose myself
In the name of loving you
This I know
I'm a burden
Heavy to maintain
But this I know
Once I love
I give out the best
And that's what hurts the most
I'm a force, ghost
Wandering in the ring of love, lost
Hopeless, rescue my soul

Yes I know
I'm hard to contain
Bu little you can take
Since I swore
And opened up the case
Now you know
This we know

I'm done

Trying to erase these moments
Cleaned this gold
And held to it
It is my wealth
But disturbs my health
It is the only language
To my world
That helps me to know
My worth
It's been years
As I've said yes
To keep it
But my mind tells me other ways
My heart poured
Itself to it
But it cracks
As it smokes away
Creating clouds
And loud sounds,
Thunderstorms
I'm done
Trying to please it
For it is the destruction
To all my doors of success
Tried to keep up to its standards
And ran crazy to all its errands
Surely I kept to its demands
By creating dangerous demons
I'm done
Appeasing it

41   A shiny heart

Glister caught my eyes
And my heart jumps out of fear
A blinking heart
Shining to my direction.
Looked at it waiting
For its election
It smiled to my reaction
The strong attraction
But the shiny heart
Found a dark-pit in my heat
And brought light
Now I glance at it
An give thank for its kindness
A shiny heart
Brought me a pack of sweets
As I devour each
Thinking of the owner of it
The owner of this shiny heart
Please come out and show yourself
For I'm patiently waiting for you
And consistently appreciate this
A heart that shows me direction
And leads me not to any temptation
The heart that brings light
To all my fights
And as I conquer them
Am grateful to have you
My warrior with a shiny heart

42 Cover

I wake up to put this balaclava
So the world cannot see
All my struggles
Fake a smile
And shine from a mile.
Milk-shake pour the iron,
My body needs revival
Cat-walk no heels on
Fooled the eyes of bishops
But any prophet can see ...
This broken vessel in me
The ghost that haunts me
Set me free
Shouts my cover
Can be my lover,
Says my heart
Lust covers my eyes
Fails to see ...
This beautiful soul
That lives as my reflection
This cover forces me to perfection
My scars hidden
And I sin in the Garden of Eden
Apple of the eye
Couldn't purify me
Your demons don't satisfy me
For you I took my soul for crucifixion
I'm glad I finally can live
With no cover
And shout, it's now over!

43   Mercy

Pour your blood
In my system
For I barely survive,
These situations
You're that drug
That gets me through
I've wronged you
I rue that day
But what's done,
Can never be taken-back
So now I beg of your mercy
These tubes are hurting
These machines make a horrible sound
I know now you're not fond
Of me
But I beg for your mercy
Rescue this orphan
I swear I'll be open
Tell you all my fears
And you'd see my tears
As they cry Mercy,
My heart bleeds
Rescue me from this bed of reeds.
Mercy … mercy … mercy
Open up your heart
And accept my request
For that's the only way I'd live

Actually it is the only path,
That I need to survive
All the storms
Even when they come in different forms
But with you I'll live

44   Soul

Dust rises
And so does seas
Some say,
It is playing
And some say it is singing
Yes life may be stinging
But sweetheart be more of the best of you
Roses can be red
But their accent it's just ironic
Let me ease your mind
You can't be perfect as much as you crave
This is more like putting a breathing soul to
grave
This is what I only have to say
I am sent to deliver this to you
And tell you, you're perfect baby
Said a pure soul
Just expressing her feelings
Tatiana Mandois
Take this my pals
It will only benefit you
And nobody else
In the world but you
Show gratitude and have your own attitude
Soul
Life's too short
For you to feel small

This world may seem round
But the corners of it are rough
Let me rest my case
For I've raised this cake
Soul, love yourself and note nobody is
perfect

45   I am learning

I am learning
To forgive
To set free
To never hold grudges
Listen to my inner messages
As they've been trying
To reach me for ages
And I've been ignorant
Turned myself to be arrogant
And longed to be heavy and big
As an elephant
To tackle all my fights
To remove this blood
That has been flowing,
Like a flood
To forgive I learn,
But my mind and heart,
Makes it hard …
To open up and forgive
So that I can set free,
This bird enclosed by my walls
The walls that has no pores
For this poor bird to escape
And tied its feet with rope
I can't let go
Mind and soul …
Rip this spirit,
For all that I wish is,
To learn to let go

46   He didn't even respond

Crippled my phone
Trying to contact him
Sent a bunch of messages
Hoping he'll respond
But no he didn't
Laying on my bed
Hoping my phone will beep
This cut me deep
As I forced myself to sleep
Convincing my mind,
His phone may be off
Maybe I'm, right
For this light
Shine bright,
To my side of bed
Wind relaxing my body
Pillow became my source
To hold on to tight
Away these unsettling thoughts
Music speaking my language
A foreign voice knows my feeling
Tears rolling down,
I am falling
Falling apart, can't contain …
This much pain
It keeps on growing
Like a baby in a womb

Can't I just pass this?
And adjust to the situation
I mean it's a secret
He's not responding
Put it to rest
That he didn't even
Respond
Like a soul lost
In an accident
He didn't respond
As I conclude that
He didn't respond
My thoughts correspond,
It is time to keep quite.

Printed in the United States
by Baker & Taylor Publisher Services